Greek Mythology

Discover the Fascinating World of Greek Gods, Heroes, Myths and Folklore

Disclaimer

This document is geared towards providing exact and reliable information in regards to the topic and issue covered. The publication is sold with the idea that the publisher is not required to render accounting, officially permitted, or otherwise, qualified services. If advice is necessary, legal or professional, a practiced individual in the profession should be ordered.

- From a Declaration of Principles which was accepted and approved equally by a Committee of the American Bar Association and a Committee of Publishers and Associations.

In no way is it legal to reproduce, duplicate, or transmit any part of this document in either electronic means or in printed format. Recording of this publication is strictly prohibited and any storage of this document is not allowed unless with written permission from the publisher. All rights reserved.

The information provided herein is stated to be truthful and consistent, in that any liability, in terms of inattention or otherwise, by any usage or abuse of any policies, processes, or directions contained within is the solitary and utter responsibility of the recipient reader. Under no circumstances will any legal responsibility or blame be held against the publisher for any reparation, damages, or monetary loss due to the information herein, either directly or indirectly.

Respective authors own all copyrights not held by the publisher.

The information herein is offered for informational purposes solely, and is universal as so. The presentation of the information is without contract or any type of guarantee assurance.

The trademarks that are used are without any consent, and the publication of the trademark is without permission or backing by the trademark owner. All trademarks and brands within this book are for clarifying purposes only and are the owned by the owners themselves, not affiliated with this document.

About This Book

This book presents the most-loved stories of Greek mythology featuring the gods and goddesses worshipped in Ancient Greece.

Most of us have heard one way or another, a story of a Greek god. Greek mythology is not only for children, but also even for adults who would like to take a respite from the real physical world and be absorbed in the powerful and mystical world of myths.

This book does just that – letting you reminisce about the stories of the gods and goddesses of Greek mythology and offering not only entertainment but also a message or two. So sit back, enjoy the book, and get lost in the magical world of Ancient Greece.

Table of Contents

Introduction

I would like to thank you for downloading this book, and I hope you will enjoy reading it as much as I enjoyed writing it!

I learned a lot about Greek mythology thanks to the bounty of literature written in Ancient Greece. Today, not many people believe in these myths, but no one can deny that stories about Greek mythology are immensely fascinating and entertaining. With all the tales of gods and goddesses, the Greeks seem to have designed mystical explanations for each occurrence in the world – natural or otherwise – and weaved these into amusing tales.

The Greeks may have lived thousands of years before us, but the influence of their myths and folklore is felt in our society even today. Take for example Cupid, who has aptly become an icon for Valentine's Day. Cupid is the god of erotic love, attraction, desire, and affection. Cupid is also the Roman equivalent of Eros, the Greek god of sexual desire and attraction. Another fine example would be Heracles, more commonly known as Hercules. The stories associated with the son of Zeus have become so common that a difficult task is often described as a "Herculean task".

Stories like these are like a pair of spectacles through which the Ancient Greeks viewed the world, to explain the unknown in the past.

I have done a great deal of research to present you with this book, and I am confident that you will love reading each page, as you get lost in the wonders of Ancient Greece.

Chapter 1:
How the World Came to Be

Scientists today say that the Big Bang Theory (the scientific theory, not the sitcom!) is the theory that best explains how the universe began. According to this theory, all the energy in the universe was inside a small dense ball, which exploded and expanded quickly. It is from this single point that all the galaxies we see today were formed. Basically, everything came from nothing.

Did you know that long before modern thinkers conceptualized the Big Bang Theory, a parallel one had been thought out by the ancient Greeks?

The ancient Greeks believed that there was a god named Chaos (which literally means "Gap"), who was a kind of an abyss without consciousness. From this abyss developed Gaia or "Mother Earth" – all complete with mountains, trees, valleys, oceans, and seas. After this formed the sky, Ouranos, that blue-in-the-day and black-in-the-night dome covering the Earth, with all its constellations of the Zodiac.

The other gods that formed from Chaos were Pontus, the first god of the Oceans, and Tartarus, the bottomless pit below the Earth. (Some stories suggest that Eros was the fourth creation of Chaos, but a few other myths claim Eros was the son of Aphrodite and Ares.). These gods are collectively known as the Primordial Deities. These are the gods from whom all the known Titans, giants, and gods descended.

Chaos and Tartarus got together and produced Nyx, the Goddess of the Night. Then Nyx had a daughter named Hemera, the Goddess of the Day. If that's not confusing enough, Gaia and Ouranus started procreating and having kids. Their first batch of kids is known as the Titans: six boys and six girls (We will go more into detail about them in the next chapter).

Their second batch of kids was the three Elder Cyclopes. The Cyclopes were big and tall like the Titans, but their most defining feature was a single eye in the center of their forehead. Ouranus was not pleased with this so they were chained and banished to the deepest pits of Tartarus.

Their third bunch was the three Hekatonkheires or "Hundred-Handed Ones". As the name makes obvious, the Hckatonkheires had a hundred arms all over their bodies. As with the Elder Cyclopes, Ouranus tossed them into Tartarus.

Gaia had a daughter and son with Tartarus and named them Echidna and Typhon. Echidna is considered the "Mother of all Monsters", while Typhon was the deadliest monster to feature in Greek mythology and is known as the "Father of all Monsters."

There were many more children of the primordial gods, but these are the ones that most commonly feature in the popular stories and myths. Basically, everything was going well until the Titans decided to castrate their father Ouranus and take over the universe!

Chapter 2:
The Castration of Ouranus

Before we begin the great saga of the first-ever castration in the universe and the events that followed during the Golden Age of the Titans (the usual stuff you know, a Titan swallowing his kids and burping them up), let's get to know who the 12 Titans were.

The 12 Titans

Cronus

Also known as Kronos, he was the youngest of the Titans, but he was their leader! He was the Titan who controlled time and sliced his father using a scythe. Cronus was the father of the Olympians.

There are many fascinating stories that revolve around this titan. He is said to have been the god of time and ruled Earth for several years. He was a hard worker and chopped crops using his sickle. He was, however, quite jealous and insecure and when he learnt of a prophecy that said his children might overthrow him, he decided not to allow any of them to live long. He ended up gobbling them live, as soon as they were born. The whole story is explained later in this book.

Rhea

Rhea is the Titan of motherhood, comfort, generation, ease, and female fertility. She was married to the Titan Cronus and was the mother of the Olympians.

Oceanus

This Titan controlled the Okeanos, a river circling Earth, which was the source of all the freshwater on the planet. The Greeks believed that when the heavenly bodies set, they descended into the water, which is why Oceanus was also believed to control their rising and setting.

Tethys

She was married to Oceanus, and was the Titan who was the source of all the freshwater on Earth. The name "Tethys" was derived from either "nurse" or "grandmother". She and her husband brought up the Titan Hera.

Hyperion

The Titan of light, he was the father of the lights of the sky. He was also the Titan of the east. His name supposedly means "he who goes above" or "watcher from above".

Theia

Theia was the wife of Hyperion and the Titan of the blue of the sky, aether and sight. Her children were Helios (the sun), Selene (the moon), and Eos (dawn).

Mnemosyne

Pronounced as "NEMO-sign", she was the Titan of remembrance and memory, mostly about learning. Take note that writing was yet to be invented in this era, so you had to remember every detail! Mnemosyne was also the inventor of words and language.

Themis

Themis was the one with the calm head who helped break up fights, which is why she was appointed as the Titan of divine law and order. She also had the gift of prophecy and controlled the Oracle of Delphi. She married Zeus and had six children. She was the first counsellor of Zeus, which gave her quite a high position.

Coeus

Spelled as Koios, he was the Titan of the north. Sometimes he was also called "Polus" as he controlled the North Pole. He was the Titan of wisdom, intelligence, and deep questions; Koios literally means "question". Coeus also had a gift of prophecy. He was known to push the limits of intelligence and was probably the wisest being to have existed at the time.

Phoebe

The Titan of thoughtful replies and wise counsel, Phoebe was married to Coeus. She had two children, Leto and Asteria, and she too held the Oracle of Delphi, which her grandson, Apollo, inherited from her. He was her second grandson, with Artemis being the first. Both were children of Leto and Zeus.

Crius

Spelled as Krios, he was the Titan of the south. He was the Titan of the constellations and his symbol was the ram, after the Aries constellation that rises in the south during springtime and was the symbol of the beginning of the Greek New Year. He married Eurybia, the daughter of the sea.

Iapetus

He was the Titan of the west and was responsible for morality and mortality. The word Iapetus means "piercer" and he was the Titan of violent death. His wife Asia was his brother, Oceanus's, daughter, and he had four sons: Prometheus, Epimetheus, Atlas and Menoetius. As Prometheus was the creator of mankind and Epimetheus was the creator of animals, Iapetus is said to be the ancestor of all mankind. His other two sons Atlas and Menoetius were said to be daring and violent, respectively.

Pandora

Epimetheus is said to have married Pandora. Pandora is famous in history for having opened the box that released all the ill things in the world.

She was created by Zeus to put an end to Prometheus's reign, as he was miffed with him for having stolen fire from the gods. He thought day and night and decided to create a beautiful maiden out of Earth and water. He then made her meet Epimetheus, who married her.

To create a ruckus in their life, Zeus gave Pandora the box as a wedding gift. It was clearly written on the box to never open it, but Zeus was sure that she would. She innocently opened it out of curiosity and it caused many problems. Some of the things that came from the box include monsters, death, illnesses etc.

But that meant nothing to the couple and they lived happy lives as they were not affected by the various things that came from the box. Eventually Pandora bore a daughter named Pyrrha. She is said to have married Deukalion, who was her cousin and son of Prometheus.

Seeing all this, Zeus was overcome by extreme anger and decided to send a huge flood down on earth. He planned to put an end to all of humanity and kill all the people on Earth with the flood. The flood is said to have wiped out a majority of people on Earth and at first, it looked as if Zeus was going to succeed in his endeavor.

But Prometheus knew of the flood and quickly warned his son Deukalion and his brother's daughter Pyrrha about it. He advised them to flee and take shelter in the high peaks of mount Parnassos. By doing so, they were able to survive the flood and were then some of the few people alive.

As soon as the floods started to go down, they approached the oracle at Delphi to seek her counsel and asked her about the future. She told them that there was still a lot of hope and that Earth was not finished.

She told them to throw their mother's bone to the ground, as it would cause people to be reborn. They were confused at first, but understood what the oracle had in mind. They both picked up stones and threw them to the ground, for their mother was Gaia. The ones that Deukalion threw turned into men and the ones that Pyrrha threw turned into women.

It is said that if Pandora had not been created, this would not have happened, and that by creating her, Zeus only helped humanity survive, which was not part of his plan.

Gaia's Wrath

Getting back to our story, Gaia was not happy and was still upset over Ouranus throwing her children into Tartarus. With the turmoil building up, she instigated her children, the Titans, to kill their father and take over the world.

According to stories, Cronus volunteered and asked his brothers to hold their father down while he cut him up with a scythe. His brothers Coeus, Crius, Hyperion and Iapetus held down Ouranus, holding each of his limbs, while Cronus castrated him and chopped him up in pieces.

When Ouranus' golden blood (ichor) splattered on the rocks, it gave birth to the three Furies, the spirits of punishment. When the ichor dropped on the fertile Earth, it gave birth to the nymphs (female deities of a particular location) and satyrs (half goats/half men).

In some myths, it is said that in order to punish Oceanus for not helping them, Cronus dropped the pieces of Ouranus into the sea, where his blood mixed with the salt water and gave birth to the Goddess Aphrodite.

After killing Ouranus, Cronus took over the world and started ruling it. At first, he freed his siblings the Elder Cyclopes and the Hekatonkheires from their prison. This pleased Gaia to no end and she went into hibernation, joyful that all her children were living happily together.

But slowly, things started going south. Cronus tossed the Elder Cyclopes and the Hekatonkheires back into Tartarus. He was a very cruel leader and all of his siblings were scared of him.

Before dying, Ouranus cursed Cronus that as he had slain his father, his children would also be the reason for his destruction. And this curse was the reason Cronus tried to avoid having children at all.

However, this plan did not succeed, so he came up with another plan. He would swallow his children whole and prevent them from overthrowing him. So when Rhea gave birth to their first child, a daughter named Hestia, he swallowed her in one big gulp. Demeter, their second daughter, met the same fate. Their third baby, again a daughter, Hera, was also swallowed by Cronus. Their fourth kid and first son Hades was swallowed in one big gulp as well. Poseidon was swallowed down too.

Rhea was hysterical. Cronus swallowed five of her kids! Though her children were immortal and couldn't be killed, she worried about them. Gaia, who was already angry with Cronus for throwing her kids back to Tartarus, spoke to her and informed her that her next child would bring her and all her children out of misery.

To save her last child from meeting a similar fate, she gave birth to Zeus on the island of Crete and offered Cronus a stone instead. Cronus blindly swallowed it, believing that he had safeguarded himself against the danger.

Zeus may have been raised by the magical goat Amalthea, although another story mentions that he was raised by a nymph named Adamanthea who protected him from Cronus by dangling him from a tree branch, suspended between his father's realms: Sky, Earth and Sea.

Once Zeus became an adult, he entered Cronus' court as a cupbearer and fed Cronus a mixture of mustard and nectar, making him throw up the contents of his stomach in reverse order. First, he threw up the stone, then Poseidon, Hades, Hera, Demeter and last Hestia. The immortal gods had been growing in his stomach.

Next, Zeus freed the Elder Cyclopes and the Hekatonkheires from their prison and had them forge weapons for him and his brothers: Zeus' lightning bolt, Poseidon's trident and Hades' helm of darkness.

What followed was known as the Titanomachy, the Titan-Olympian war. Let us look at this war closely in order to comprehend better exactly what happened between the Titans and Olympians.

Chapter 3:
Titanomachy In Greek mythology

Titanomachy is ancient Greek is a ten year period when nothing but battle was the order of the day. This period is what we refer to as the very infamous clash of the Titans. It happened in a series of battles fought in Thessaly. The battle was between the older generation gods/titans based out of Mount Othrys, and the younger generation of Olympian gods who later come to rest their reign on Mount Olympus. Mainly, the raging ten-year battle had one intention: to decide which school of gods would have a domain over the universe. The Olympians emerged victorious.

Those who lived during this age tell tales and poems of the war between the titans and the gods. More specifically, the most dominant one and perhaps the only one that survived is the Theogony that has attribtions to Hesoid. Titanomachia, a lost epic, has attributions to the blind Thracian bard Tharmvris, who is himself a legendary figure on his own (there is mention of him in an essay of music attributed to Plutarch). Further, titans also played a major role in the disbursement of poems attributed to Orpheus. Sadly, only bits of the Orphic narrative survived history. However, the little there is shows major differences from the Hesiodic tradition.

Event leading to the war

As every major battle in history, the clash of the titans has some important background information that we should look at.

Majorly, the battle stage for this war happened when Cronos, the youngest titan successfully overthrew Uranus, his father, who was at the time the ruler of the cosmos and the heavens itself. Cronos had help from his mother Gaia who was miffed by Uranus for imprisoning her children Cyclopesin and Hecatonchires in Tartarus. It is said that Gaia created a great sickle and gathered Cronus and his brothers hoping to convince them that castrating Uranus was necessary. In this meeting, only Cronus rose to the task. Gaia gave him the sickle and planned an ambush.

Folklore has it that at the next meeting between Gaia and Uranus, Cronus attacked Uranus and used the sickle to castrate him by cutting off his genitals and casting them into the sea and becoming king in the process. However, before his death, Uranus made a prophecy that the seed of Cronus aka his children would rebel against him and overthrow him just like he did his father. The spill of Uranus blood saw the rise of Meliae, Gigantes, and Erinyes. His cut genitals and semen saw the rise of Aphrodite from the sea.

After castrating his father and taking over power, Cronus cemented his power on the throne by re-imprisoning his brothers in Tartarus.

Due to his paranoia and fear of an end to his rule, Cronus became a terrible king, worse than his farther. He swallowed his children whole as soon as his wife Rhea bore them. Nevertheless, Rhea hid one son, her youngest son, Zeus by tricking Cronus into swallowing disguised as a baby by wrapping it in a blanket.

Rhea, fearing for her son's life, took him to a cave in Crete and gave him to Amalthea to raise as hers. As a young adult, Zeus masqueraded as Cronus' cupbearer and once he cemented himself as a servant of Cronus, Metis gave him a portion; a portion of wine and mustard to administer to Cronus and one that would make him vomit all the children he had swallowed.

After freeing his brother and sisters, he, Zeus, led them in a massive rebellion against the titans. His siblings were disgorged. Zeus waged a war against his father with his siblings Hestia, Poseidon, Hera, Hades, and Demeter. He also freed the Cyclopes and the Hecatonchires from where they were imprisoned by Cronus. The latter allied with Zeus against Cronus. The most iconic powers Zeus had (lightning, and thunder) were gifts from the Cyclopes, while the Hecathonchires helped fight the battle hurling stones. Cronus had some allies; he was not fighting the war alone. On his side were all the other titans except for Prometheus and Themis who fought on the side of Zeus. A key personnel on the Cronus side of the war was Atlas. After ten years of war and battle, Zeus and the other Olympians won and imprisoned the Titans in Tartarus with the Hecatonchires as their guards. Atlas was punished for his deeds by being made to hold up the sky. According to some accounts, Zeus was a different ruler. After cementing his power, he reluctantly offered the imprisoned titans their freedom.

If we were to follow Hyginus, the main cause of the Titanomachy would be as follows; "After Hera saw the power that Epaphus, who was born of a concubine, wielded by ruling Egypt (a great kingdom), she made sure that he was murdered while he was out hunting. She encouraged the titans to drive Zeus out of the kingdom and have power given back to Cronus. When they attempted to climb heaven, Zeus, Artemis, Apollo, and Athena cast them into Tartarus. Because Atlas was their leader, he put the vault on the sky, where he is said to be even today, holding up the sky on his shoulders.

After emerging victorious after the war, the three brothers took a lot with Zeus becoming the ruler of the sky and the air. Poseidon chose the sea and all universal waters, while Hades received the underworld and the entire realm of the dead. All the other gods received powers in accordance with proclivities of each and nature. The earth became a realm for all and none to do with as they pleased unless a dispute arose and the three main brothers had to intervene.

A Titanomachy poem

In ancient Greek, Titanomachy is an epic poem depicting the struggles that Zeus and the other Olympian gods had in overthrowing Cronus and what was then his divine generation i.e. the Titans, who then were traditionally affiliated to Eumelus of Corinth. Eumelus was a legendary bard belonging to the Bacchiard ruling family in archaic Corinth and who was a treasured composer of the Prosodion. Prosodion was the processional anthem performed by Delos during Messenian independence.

Even as an antiquity, there are those who cite the Titanomachia as without a name. A professional in Greek mythology, M.L West, concluded that the name Eumelos attachment to the poem was only because it was the only name available. Because the evidence is patchy, some conclude that the Titanomachy accounts of Eumelos differed with those of the surviving account of Hesiod's Theogony at salient point. The Titanomachy later become two books, the battle of Olympians and Titans, which was preceded by a sort of genealogy or theogony of primeval gods. In this the theogony, Lydus, the late roman writer remarked that the writer of the Titanomachy placed the birth of Zeus in Lydia, rather than in Crete.

Chapter 4:
The Olympians

After the fall of the Titans, the Olympians took over the world. Theirs was a very prosperous era, and it was in this era that humans (who were just puny insects for the Titans) started evolving and gaining more importance.

The 15 Greatest Olympians

Let's look at each of the major gods (who appear in a lot of the stories) in greater detail and learn about the stories associated with them.

Hestia

Hestia was the eldest child of Cronus and Rhea, the first to be swallowed and the last to be disgorged. Hestia was the goddess of the hearth. She was a virgin goddess and she had sworn on Zeus' head to never marry. Maybe this was why Zeus valiantly protected her from her many ardent suitors. She was a kind goddess and gave up her throne on the council of the Olympians for Dionysus. She was the symbol of the relationship between the different colonies and cities.

Demeter

The second daughter of the Titans Cronus and Rhea, Demeter, was the goddess of fertility and agriculture. Demeter had a daughter named Persephone with Zeus. When Poseidon tried to seduce her, she turned into a mare to escape him, but Poseidon turned into a stallion and mounted her, and she had twins from this encounter: a girl named Desponia, the goddess of horses, and Arion, an immortal horse. Her last child was from a mortal man named Iasion. She gave birth to Plutous, the minor god of agricultural health.

A very popular story that shows the wrath of Demeter is the story of Erisikthon. Erisikthon was a prince who decided to make a palace of wood, and the wood was to be taken from Demeter's sacred grove. Demeter did not take too kindly to this and cursed him with never-ending hunger and thirst, to the extent that when his money ran out, he ended up eating his own flesh to satiate his hunger.

Persephone

The daughter of Zeus and Demeter, she is perhaps one of the most famous minor goddesses. She was the goddess of springtime. The story goes that Hades fell in love with her while she played in the meadow with her companions, the Oceanids (the daughters of Oceanus). Hades kidnapped her and took her to his underground realm forcibly.

When Demeter knew this, she was really angry and starved the entire world. No crops would grow and mortals started dying. To prevent this from continuing for too long, Zeus and/or Hermes (there are stories about both) struck up a bargain between Demeter and Hades. Persephone would spend two thirds each year with Demeter above ground and one third of the year with Hades in his underground realm. This story was used as an explanation for why nothing grows in winter, because that is when Persephone is with Hades and Demeter is in mourning!

Hera

The youngest daughter of Cronus and Rhea, Hera was the goddess of marriage, women, motherhood, and childbirth. She was also Zeus' wife and the queen of Olympus. Hera married Zeus and bore three kids from the marriage – Ares, the god of war, Hebe, the goddess of eternal youth, and Eileithyia, the goddess of childbirth.

The marriage of Zeus and Hera was built on deceit. Zeus tried to win Hera's heart on multiple occasions. However, he was unsuccessful because of Hera's lack of interest. So, he took the form of a disheveled cuckoo and entered her room through an open window. When Hera saw the bird, being the kind goddess she was, she decided to help it. She kept it between her breasts and tried to keep it warm. Zeus transformed into his human self at this point and caught Hera by surprise. Taking advantage of Hera's momentary lapse, Zeus raped her. She ended up agreeing to the marriage to cover up this lascivious and disrespectful act.

Their marriage was the perfect recipe for disaster. Hera was not pleased with Zeus' many marriages and affairs and decided to revolt against him. She realized she was not alone in this. Other gods felt oppressed by Zeus and wanted to overthrow him. Hera gave Zeus a drug, which he consumed unknowingly. The other gods helped Hera in binding him to the couch. However, they had no idea as to what to do next. While they kept arguing in front of the couch, Briareus, who was once saved by Zeus, sneaked silently into the room and went near the couch unnoticed by the other gods and Hera. He untied Zeus from the couch. When Zeus got up with a lightning bolt in his hand, the other gods got scared of him and went on their knees pleading him to forgive them. Zeus, who was enraged grabbed Hera by the hair and hung her from the sky with the aid of golden chains. Not able to bear the pain, Hera kept weeping the whole night, which kept Zeus up. The other gods, despite feeling sorry for Hera, were not in a position to help her. Next morning, Zeus promised to release her from the shackles if she promised to not plot against him in the future. With no other choice left, she accepted his offer and promised never to rebel against him. She did keep her word but she never stopped voicing her displeasure.

Tired of watching Zeus sire children with nymphs, mortals, other goddesses, titans and even himself, Hera decided to have a child by herself. Through sheer determination, she bore Hephaestus all by herself. But with one look at him, she realized how big of a mistake that was! Hephaestus was terribly deformed and she threw him off Olympus. For being a goddess of motherhood, she was kind of evil, wasn't she?

Hades

Hades was the eldest male Olympian by birth, but the most junior as he was the last to be regurgitated. He was the Lord of the Underworld, god of the dead and all the riches below the Earth. Despite being one of the elder Gods, Hades was not on the Olympian council and rarely left his realm.

How Hades became the lord of the underworld was a matter of luck. When Cronus was overthrown by his sons, Poseidon, Zeus and Hades, they decided to determine the successor to the throne by drawing lots. Hades picked up the lot containing the Underworld and thus he became its god.

Hades' weapon from the Elder Cyclopes was his Helm of Darkness, which rendered him invisible and broadcast waves of pure terror. His realm had five rivers: Cocytus (the river of wailing), Phlegethon (the river of fire), Acheron (the river of pain), Lethe (the river of forgetfulness), and Styx (the river of hate).

The Underworld had three levels for the dead: Elysium (the heaven of Underworld, with the Island of the Blest for people who achieved Elysium in three different lifetimes), the Fields of Asphodel (the place for average people, who were neither good nor bad), and the Fields of Punishment (the hell of the Underworld, where all the evil spirits went).

One of the most famous and creative tortures by Hades was for Tantalus, the Greek king who invited the gods for dinner and served them stew made from the flesh of his children! As a punishment, Tantalus was to stand in a pool of water up to his waist, below a tree bearing fruit, but he could not eat or drink a thing! How is that for punishment?

Hades eventually fell in love with Persephone and abducted her to stay with him in the Underworld. He married her shortly after her abduction.

But Hades is extremely misunderstood. He is often compared to the devil and said to have bad intent. Given his reputation of collecting people after death, he is regarded as being the evil one. However, he is only doing his duty. Anybody who was in his position would have done the same!

There is also the instance of him having let go of Orpheus' wife when he entered the Underworld to save her.

Orpheus' wife was Eurydice. She was the daughter of Apollo. He was immensely in love with her and is said to have played music day and night during their wedding.

One day, a demigod named Aristaeous started pursuing her after he saw her and was taken by her beauty. Eurydice began running from him and he started chasing her. She then trod on a serpent and was bitten. The bite was so potent that she immediately died and went to the Underworld.

Orpheus was so sad that he started singing sad songs and played his instruments out of grief. The gods were taken aback by his grief and wept with him. They advised him to go to the Underworld and persuade Hades to free his bride.

He made his way there and began to persuade Hades with his soulful songs. Hades had his initial doubts, but decided to allow Eurydice to go back to the upper world because she had someone who loved her so religiously.

However, he proposed that Orpheus lead the way and that he should not look back to see her, until they reached the upper world safely. If he failed to do so, then he would not be rewarded with Eurydice.

Delighted at the proposal, both of them left the Underworld and Orpheus led his bride.

He is said to have travelled for a long time, full of joy. However, as the upper world approached, he started doubting Eurydice's presence. He wondered if he was being fooled, just so that he would go away from the Underworld. Just as he approached the upper world, he decided to see if she was there and the light of the sun fell on her face.

The minute he turned back, she disappeared and fell back into the Underworld.

It is clear that Hades did not have any bad intentions. Besides, he was not the judge of who should die, which was completely the choice of the demigods Minos, Aiakos and Rhadamanthys.

Poseidon

The second eldest son of Rhea and Cronus (either way – by birth or by barf), was the god of the sea, earthquakes and horses. He was also known as the "Earth-Shaker". Poseidon was married to the Nereid Amphitrite, but like his brother Zeus, he had many affairs and thus many children.

With Amphitrite, he had three children Triton and two daughters, Rhodes and Benthesicyme. He had two children with his sister Demeter. Poseidon even courted Medusa (who was turned into a gorgon by Athena) and when Perseus cut off her head, her two children with Poseidon, Pegasus (the winged horse) and Chrysoar, sprang out of her neck. He even mingled with mortal women and fathered some of the famous heroes, including Theseus, the Athenian hero, Ancaeus, a hero who sailed with Jason, and Ephemeus, an important Argonaut. He also is said to have fathered most of the younger Cyclopes.

Poseidon contested against Athena to be the patron god of Athens. He produced a spectacular saltwater spring, while Athena made the first olive tree. He lost by a very small margin.

Zeus

Zeus was the youngest Olympian by birth, but was considered the eldest (he was never swallowed.) Cronus, who feared that his children would overthrow him, swallowed each of his children as soon as they were born. Rhea, who was heartbroken, decided to save at least Zeus. She tricked Cronus into swallowing a stone instead of Zeus. That is how Zeus was later able to save his siblings.

Zeus was the Lord of the Sky and the king of the gods. Zeus had three wives. His first wife was Metis, whom he swallowed because he feared a prophecy that claimed his own son would overthrow him. His second wife was the Titan Themis, who bore him two sets of triplets: the Horai (the seasons) and the three Fates. His third and final wife, as mentioned earlier, was Hera.

Zeus had many children. His godly children with Hera were Ares, Hebe and Eileithyia. He had twins from the Titan Leto, Apollo and Artemis. He had Hermes with a Pleiad named Maia and Persephone with Demeter. And that was just his heavenly kids. He had Minos with the mortal princess Europa, Perseus with Danae, and Heracles with Alcmene. He even had Athena all by himself!

He is said to have been extremely involved with several women and went to great lengths to sleep with them. He indulged in rape and forced himself on women of all ages. He is said to have changed himself into animals just to get women to sleep with him. At one point in time, he is said to have seduced a mother and daughter together, who happened to be his brother's wife and her mother. He impregnated both women. There were just so many of his children running around!

Being the king of the gods, Zeus was widely feared by immortals and mortals alike. Greeks honored every traveler, every beggar, and every old person they came across, because Zeus had the habit of disguising himself and incinerating those who were unkind to him!

Athena

So, Zeus swallowed Metis and Metis gave birth to Athena inside Zeus. Metis faded into pure thought, but Athena continued growing in Zeus' gut. Zeus had a terrible headache and Hephaestus split his skull open and out popped Athena in full armor! This is probably why some myths suggest that Athena did not have a mother and was born out of Zeus. Athena soon became the favorite child of Zeus. Athena was the goddess of crafts, warfare, and wisdom. She was a maiden goddess and never married.

The most famous story related to Athena was of her competition with the weaver Arachne. Arachne was a weaver from Lydia with extraordinary talent. People from all over the kingdom would go to her house to watch her spin out beautiful tapestries. In her pride, she claimed she was a better weaver than Athena herself. This displeased Athena and she challenged her to a weaving contest. Arachne lost and Athena turned her into a spider as a punishment for being too proud. Even today, spiders are known as Arachnids.

One of the things that made Athena a strong warrior was her strategic planning capabilities. She was successful in all the battles in which she participated purely because of her strategies. Athena was worshipped as the patron of the city of Athens. She was also the goddess of agriculture and handicraft. Her many inventions include the pot, the bridle, the trumpet, the flute, the rake, the ship, the plow, the chariot and the yoke.

The holy tree of Athena was the olive tree while her holy bird was the owl.

Aphrodite

She was technically a Titan, born when Ouranus' parts were dropped into the sea. She was the goddess of love and beauty and was married to Hephaestus. She was known to have many affairs, the most famous one being with Ares. She gave birth to Anteros (Passion), Eros (Love, though some stories claim Eros was born out of Chaos), Deimos (Fear), Phobos (Panic) and Harmonia, wife of Cadmus of Thebes, with Ares.

Even her husband knew of her affairs, and he often set up traps to catch her in the act with one of her lovers. He once caught the lovers naked in a net in his bedchamber and invited the Olympians to mock them.

She had a son, Aeneas, with a mortal king named Anchises. Aeneas survived the Trojan War and went on to lay the foundation for the Roman Empire.

A lesser-known fact about Aphrodite is that she was interested in military affairs as well. She is popular for her beauty, no doubt, but she was also famous for her military aspirations. However, she was not interested in taking charge and leading armies into battle.

Ares

He was the eldest son of Hera and Zeus and was the god of war. It was said that when Ares walked onto the battlefield, his companions Phobos (fear) and Deimos (terror) always accompanied him. His union with his sister Aphrodite resulted in the birth of Phobos, Deimos and Eris (goddess of discord).

Ancient Greeks did not worship Ares much; after all, who likes war? Well, there was one exception, the city of Sparta. The Spartans kept a statue of Ares chained in their city so that the god would never desert them and they would always find the courage to fight wars. Go figure.

However, not many know of Ares' real nature. He was worshipped for his bravery and ability to take on several super powers in war, but that is very different from what he really was. Ares was the god of war, no doubt, but he was not in the least brave. He always used Athena, his sister, as a shield, and the countless victories that he had were only because of her.

He is said to have been a big coward, and his family despised him. They were not supportive of him always whining and crying about going to wars and taking on super powers.

The time that he took on his sister, Athena, in a war, he is said to have lost badly. He was then chased away from the battlefield by his father who was completely humiliated by his son.

Hephaestus

He was the son of Hera alone and was supposedly so ugly that his own mother threw him off Mount Olympus, an action that crippled him. Hephaestus was the god of the forge, fire and metalwork and he took revenge on his mother by presenting her with a throne that bound her to it with a golden fetter. He only released her after Dionysus got him drunk.

He did not have any kids with his wife Aphrodite, but had twins with a sea nymph named Kabeiro, known as the Kabeiroi. They were a lot like their father and helped him at his forges.

Apollo

Apollo was the son of Zeus and Leto. The birth of Apollo (and his twin Artemis) is quite an interesting story. Their mother, the Titan Leto, was pregnant with the twins when Hera issued a warning to all the landmasses with roots to Gaia that none of them should let Leto give birth on them. Leto searched the whole planet for land that would let her give birth, but all refused. Leto finally went to Delos, a floating island, and gave birth to the twins.

Apollo was the god of music, youth, archery, prophecy, and healing. He also took over from the Titan Helios and became the god of the Sun. He controlled the Oracle of Delphi. Though he did not marry, he had many affairs. Since he was the god of healing, there are many tales that speak about his healing powers. However, he was also capable of bringing about deadly diseases and plagues by shooting his arrows.

Artemis

Apollo's twin sister was a maiden goddess and the goddess of wild animals and childbirth. She took over the Titan Selene's duty and became the Goddess of the Moon. Artemis was a huntress and had a band of followers known as the "Hunters of Artemis". They were young maidens who were granted immortality on the condition that they would remain virgins for life.

She was the goddess of chastity, virginity and the hunt. She was granted eternal virginity by her father, Zeus, at her request. Her lifetime was spent in hunting and protecting nature. She was also responsible for agriculture and animal herding. It is said that there were many suitors who wanted the hand of Artemis in marriage but she was successful in eluding them all. However, it is said in one myth that she lost her heart to Orion, who was her hunting partner.

There are some lesser-known stories in regard to Artemis that claim her to have been ruthless. She was referred to as the Lion by her stepmother Hera. She was proud of the name and showed no compassion towards anybody who defied her or her family.

There are stories of her having killed several women. The most popular account is of Artemis having killed six daughters of Niobe; Niobe had ruffled her feathers when she went around boasting that she had more children than Leto. Artemis is also said to have killed Iphigenia as revenge for her father's killing of a deer in a sacred grove.

Hermes

Hermes was the son of Zeus and Maia, a Pleiad. Hermes was a god with many roles. He was the god of thieves, messenger of the gods, and the god of travelers, sports, border crossings, and athletes. Just after his birth in a cave, he stole some of Apollo's sacred cows. When Apollo realized his cows were missing, he got really angry. In order to placate him, Hermes invented the lyre and gave it to Apollo. Hermes carried a caduceus, which was like a shepherd's staff with two intertwining snakes on it. He is known for his trademark winged-helmet and winged-shoes. Hermes never married, but had many mistresses.

Dionysus

He was the son of Zeus and Semele. When Hera killed Semele, Zeus saved the unborn Dionysus by sewing him into his thigh and protecting him. Dionysus means "born twice". Dionysus was the god of wine, grapes, and ecstasy.

Dionysus invented wine with his friend, the nymph Silenus. Dionysus had a throng of followers and his female followers were known as Maenads. It is said that to make room for him on the Olympian council, Hestia gave up her place, hence misbalancing the male god to female god ratio on the council.

Chapter 5:
Heroes

Every story needs a hero! Greek mythology is no exception. The heroes played an important role in the Greek pantheon. Some of them were as powerful as a god, yet mortal. Let us look at the various heroes who ruled the hearts of the Greeks and their gods in this chapter.

Atlanta

There is hardly any record that might give us an idea about the parents of Atlanta. However, when she was born, Atlanta was abandoned by her father and left to die in the deadly forest. It was suggested that the reason behind her father's action was because having a girl child was considered a disgrace to the royal family.

Atlanta was brought up by a bear in the forest. She soon found herself associated with many hunters and became one of the best hunters in the history of the Greeks. She was exceptionally good at archery. There are many tales about her skill as an archer.

She was also considered the fastest mortal on earth. There is an interesting tale surrounding this ability. When Atlanta grew up, her father was ashamed of abandoning her as a child and accepted her into the kingdom. As was his duty, he decided to find an apt suitor for her and get her married. However, Atlanta, who was keen on remaining a virgin, came up with a foolproof idea to save herself from the hassles of getting married. She came up with a test and promised to marry whoever completed it. You may have guessed as to what the test was! She would marry the person who beat her in a footrace. As expected, there was no one who could outrun the fastest mortal on earth.

Her plan continued to work and she was successful in guarding her virginity until Melanion came into the picture. Melanion was hopelessly in love with Atlanta and somehow wanted to win her heart and hand in marriage. But he knew he could never win the race without some help, so he prayed to goddess Aphrodite to help him out in this impossible task. Aphrodite, who was always kind towards lovers, offered her help to Melanion. She gave him three golden apples and a plan that would help him. In return for the help, Melanion was supposed to sacrifice to Aphrodite.

When the race between the two began, Melanion tossed a golden apple when Atlanta tried to gain a lead. Atlanta got distracted and out of sheer overconfidence stopped to pick the apple. Melanion did this the next time she got ahead as well. But being the fastest mortal, despite these distractions, Atlanta had almost regained the lead when they neared the finishing line. However, when Melanion threw in the final apple, Atlanta got distracted and Melanion won the race. And Atlanta then had no choice but to marry him.

Despite her initial hesitance about getting married, she enjoyed the marriage. However, it was not a happy fairy tale ending for Atlanta and Melanion. Melanion, engrossed in the joys of married life, forgot about the promise he had given to Aphrodite.

When Melanion and Atlanta entered a shrine to pray to its deity, Aphrodite cursed them with overpowering desire. Forgetting where they were, Melanion and Atlanta made love in the shrine itself. This angered the deity and they were both transformed into lions.

Bellerophon

Bellerophon was the son of Poseidon and Eurynome. However he was brought up by Glaucus. Bellerophon's quest in capturing Pegasus could possibly be attributed to both Poseidon and Glaucus' interests in horses.

Bellerophon was able to capture and tame the winged steed with the help of a magical bridle gifted to him by Athena. He was sent on a number of deadly tasks by King Iobates. The first stop on the deadly adventure was to slay Chimaera, which he did with the help of Pegasus. He went on to conquering the Solymi tribe next. After this was a daring battle against the Amazons, and Bellerophon again emerged victorious. He was not only a brave warrior but also a skillful archer. He was offered the hand of Philonoe, the daughter of King Iobates, in marriage as a reward for his bravery. Hippolochus, Isander, Deidameia and Laodameia were his children.

However, the good times lasted only till Bellerophon let his pride overtake him. He, who was favored by gods, decided to ride to Mount Olympus on Pegasus. It was an attempt to shame the Olympian gods. His pride was his downfall. Zeus interrupted him during his climb to Mount Olympus and he was dismounted. He fell down, and although he survived, Bellerophon was crippled for life.

Heracles

Heracles, also known as Hercules, was the strongest of all mortals. He was even stronger than some of the gods. He was the last mortal son of Zeus.

Heracles' strength helped the gods win their war against the giants. Even though he was a strong warrior, he lacked greatly in the intellect department. He was regarded as foolish by many. Once, he was so annoyed by the heat that he threatened to kill the sun with his arrow. He took offense at things very easily and quickly. He formed grudges at the drop of a hat and never made an effort to forgive people. The club was his favorite weapon. He was known to have worn a lion skin with the head attached as a garment. His mindless acts were the reason for most of his problems.

Not many people know that the popular saying "taking the bull by the horns" can be traced to Heracles — he is said to have fought a bull to atone for killing his wife and children.

Meleager

Meleager was the son of Althaea and King Oeneus of Calydon. The Fates, Clotho, Atropos and Lachesis, foretold his future within seven days of his birth. Lachesis and Clotho predicted that Meleager would grow up to be a brave lad and would be known for his nobility. On the other hand, Atropos warned him about his death. It was prophesized that Meleager would die as soon as a certain stick in the fireplace burnt up completely. To save her son's life, Althaea pulled out that stick and hid it.

His bravery helped him to kill King Aeetes, who was the main enemy of the Argonauts. He married Cleopatra Alcyone after this victorious task. Their daughter was Polydora. Meleager would have led a happily-ever-after life if not for Artemis. Artemis' handiwork resulted in a deadly boar ravaging the lands of Meleager, who along with the other brave huntsmen in his land set out to hunt and kill it. This was the infamous Calydonian BoarHunt. However, this was the downfall of Meleager as well, bringing about his death. There are different stories about his death but it is safe to say that it all started with the Calydonian BoarHunt!

Perseus

Perseus was the son of Zeus and Danae. There is an interesting story as to how Perseus was born. Danae was the daughter of King Acrisius. It was prophesized by the Oracle of Apollo that the son of Danae would kill him. Fearing this, he locked his daughter up in a tower made out of bronze. This way, nobody could marry her and there was no possibility of Danae having children.

This plan was working just fine for Acrisius until the gods intervened. The cell in which Danae was locked up in the tower had no doors. There was only a little window through which she could see the outside world. One day, a man appeared at the window and he was carrying a thunderbolt in his hand. Well, it was Zeus indeed who appeared at Danae's window. He transformed the entire prison to look as lovely as luscious gardens, which made Danae happy. He also voiced his intention of making Danae his wife.

When Acrisius noticed the light and brightness the room was emitting, he suspected foul play and asked his guards to tear open one of the walls. When he entered the room, he found Danae playing happily with a baby on her lap. Angered by Danae's action and out of fear that the prophecy might come true, Acrisius locked both Danae and her son inside a big chest and threw it into the sea for them to die there. However, they both survived and sought refuge in the island of Seriphos, which was being ruled by Polydectes. As we all know, the baby grew up to be the brave Perseus.

Many tales stand testimony to the bravery of Perseus. But there is another interesting story as to how he set out on those daring tasks. It was believed that Polydectes wanted to marry Danae but Perseus was being a hindrance to his plan. He knew that unless he got rid of Perseus, there was no hope left for him. He came up with a plan to achieve this. Polydectes announced that he would be marrying the daughter of his friend. The customary practice during those days was that every subject of his land had to give him a wedding gift. And accordingly, everybody came to visit the king and gave him their wedding gifts, except Perseus. Perseus could not afford a gift because of his poverty. This seemed to infuriate Polydectes. Perseus, who did not want to hurt Polydectes' feelings, offered to get him anything from any part of the world. Expecting Perseus to fall for this trap, Polydectes presented him with the most impossible of tasks, hoping that Perseus would die trying to accomplish it. He asked Perseus to give him the head of Medusa. It was a well-known fact that anybody who looked into the eyes of Medusa would turn into stone instantly. Accepting this feat would be equivalent to walking to his death. However, Perseus accepted it and set out on this adventure.

With the help of his siblings, Athena and Hermes, and the Nymphs of the North, Perseus was successful in beheading Medusa. He carried the head of Medusa in a magical bag to make sure that he didn't see her eyes. During his return to Seriphos, he also ended up saving Andromeda. Andromeda was apparently chained to a rock and was left to die at the hands of a sea monster sent by Poseidon. Perseus saved her from the sea monster. When he took her back to her father, King Cepheus, he asked for her hand in marriage. With the consent of the king, they married and set out to Seriphos.

On their way home, they took part in several other games as well. In one of those events, when Perseus threw a discus, it ended up hitting an old man and killing him. The old man was none other than king Acrisius. The prophecy indeed came true.

When Perseus and Andromeda reached Seriphos, he learnt that Polydectes had shamed his mother by making her his handmaid when she had refused to marry him. Angered by this, Perseus entered the court and held out the head of Medusa. All Polydectes had to do was look at her eyes, and it is not so difficult to guess what happened next!

Perseus and Andromeda continued to rule happily and had many descendants who played an important part in Greek mythology. However, Perseus eventually met his death at the hands of Dionysus. It is believed that Perseus and Andromeda were transformed into stars to stay with each other for eternity.

Theseus

Theseus was a Greek hero who was well known for his strength, courage, intelligence, and wisdom. His many adventures not only ended up glorifying him but also greatly benefitted Athens. He played an important role in the consolidation of Athenian power with his shrewd political tactics. The ideology of democracy first came into existence because of Theseus. He was considered the champion of the oppressed and the poor.

The Athenians loved Theseus for his wisdom and knowledge. However, this did not last long. Theseus started losing his wisdom as he grew older. Bad decisions and foolish adventures became a major part of Theseus' life, and Athens saw his reputation going downhill. People of Athens started disrespecting him for his senseless actions. Eventually Theseus died in exile. The people of Athens did not even bother to bring back his body and give him a proper funeral.

That is seen as being his punishment for having abandoned his father and a princess.

In happier times, he was celebrated as a hero for having saved several people in Crete from being killed by the Minotaur. He is said to have bravely gone in and fought the Minotaur but what most people don't realize is that he did not do it alone.

His helper was Ariadne, who was the king's daughter. She is said to have fallen for him and he might have promised her marriage only to get her help.

King Minos had set up a big maze that was quite difficult to get through. There were a lot of twists and turns and many had tried and failed. The maze was designed by Diadaloz and is said to have been the most difficult of mazes to solve at the time.

Ariadne handed Theseus a ball of golden wool, which is said to have helped in finding his way out of the maze. He had promised Ariadne that he would marry her, and carried her with him outside of Crete.

However, as soon as they reached the island of Naxos, he is said to have abandoned her and moved on.

She was heartbroken, but given his history of fathering several children by different women and abandoning them all, it was nothing new. In fact, he had raped a lot of these women and they lived in fear of him.

He had been asked by his father to turn his sail to red once he got safely away from Crete, to signal that he was safe. He forgot to do so and his father committed suicide out of grief.

Chapter 6:
Greek Mythical Creatures

Many fiction and fantasy book writers have drawn inspiration from Greek mythology. Perhaps when you finish reading this chapter, you will realize how many of the various monsters you came across in your childhood fantasy books were actually taken from Greek myths.

In this chapter, we describe many exciting mythical creatures of the Greek pantheon.

Argus Panoptes

Argus Panoptes was a giant who had eyes all over his body. It is said that he had about one hundred eyes. He was also known as Argos. While serving the goddess Hera, he was entrusted with the responsibility of slaying the monster Echidna. He emerged victorious from this deadly task. His main responsibility for Hera was to guard Io. Io was a nymph with whom Zeus was having an affair. Zeus was unable to get past Argos because Argos was capable of detecting any sort of movement with the help of his hundred eyes. Zeus finally took the aid of Hermes to assist him with this. Hermes disguised himself as a shepherd and put Argos into a deep slumber. He killed him with a stone as soon as he went to sleep.

Ash Tree Nymphs

The Ash Tree Nymphs were also known as the Meliae. When Cronus castrated Ouranus to remove him from power, a few drops of his blood fell on earth. The Ash Tree Nymphs (along with the giants and the Erinyes) are believed to have come into existence from these blood drops.

It was believed that the Ash Tree Nymphs were the ancestors of Bronze Age man.

Centaurs

Centaurs were half-horse / half-human creatures. Their torso, arms and head resembled those of a man whereas the body resembled that of a horse. Centaurs were considered the children of Nephele and Ixion. However, another myth suggests that centaurs were born when Centaurus mated with the Magnesian mares.

Centaurs were considered lustful, wild creatures. Chiron was the only centaur who did not fall under this general description. He was wise and modest. He was well known for his knowledge in the field of medicine and his capabilities as a teacher.

He was the tutor of Achilles, Aesculapius and many other prominent people who lived in Greece at the time. He was an immortal centaur. However, Heracles accidentally wounded him with an arrow that was dipped in the blood of the monster Hydra. Since Chiron was immortal, he did not suffer death from the poison in the arrow. However, the wound persisted and brought him a lot of pain.

Chiron ultimately sacrificed his life to save Prometheus and to put an end to the pain he was suffering from.

Cerberus

Cerberus was a three-headed dog. He was the son of Echidna and Typhon. He was entrusted with the responsibility of guarding the entrance to the Underworld. He would allow the dead to enter the Underworld but would not let anyone leave it. Even more fearsome than his three heads were his other physical attributes, like a serpent's tail, lion's claws, and a mane that was made up of snakes.

Chimaera

Chimaera was another child of Echidna and Typhon. Its siblings were Cerberus and the Lernean Hydra. The head and body of the Chimaera were those of a lion while its tail ended with the head of a snake. Apart from that, the head of a goat was affixed to its back. Chimaera could be described as the only hybrid monster in Greek mythology.

Chimaera inhabited the region of Lycia and savaged the entire land by breathing out fire. As mentioned earlier, king Iobates who was ruling over this region sent out Bellerophon to slay Chimaera. With the help of Pegasus and his exceptional archery, Bellerophon was successful in slaying Chimaera.

Chrysaor

Chrysaor was the brother of Pegasus, the winged horse. He was also the son of Poseidon and Medusa. It was believed that Pegasus and Chrysaor came into existence when Medusa was decapitated. Even though there is not much record of Chrysaor's involvement in Greek mythology, he was well known for being a firm-hearted warrior.

Cyclopes

The Cyclopes were humongous monsters that had only one eye. According to one myth, the parents of the Cyclopes were Uranus and Gaea. However, another account suggests that they were the sons of Poseidon.

The Cyclopes were equivalent to the giants in terms of strength and growth. Their one eye was situated in the middle of their foreheads. The Cyclopes were neither god-fearing nor followers of the laws of the nature. They were the rulers of themselves. They were employed by Hephaestus, who had his workshop in the heart of the volcano Etna.

Polyphemus was the chief representative of the Cyclopes. It was believed that Odysseus was responsible for outwitting and blinding Polyphemus. Apparently, Polyphemus fell in love with Galatea, who was a mesmerizing nymph. It was only natural that she did not love this grotesque monster back, especially since she was already in love with a youth named Acis. Angered by her rejection, Polyphemus killed Acis by throwing a gigantic rock upon him, which unsurprisingly crushed him to death.

Literary accounts describe only three other prominent Cyclopes. They were Steropes (lightning), Brontes (thunder) and Arges (thunderbolt). They were also known as the storm gods, and they became the first smiths. When Cronus overthrew his father Uranus and became king, one of the first few things he did was condemning the Cyclopes to Tartarus. When the fight between the Titans and the Olympians broke out, Zeus released them from the Underworld and allowed them to fight for the Olympians. As a token of gratitude for freeing them, the Cyclopes gifted their weapons of thunder and lightning to Zeus. They spent the remainder of their lives serving the Olympian gods at Mount Olympus.

Echidna

Echidna was a Greek monster who had the torso and head of a woman while the lower part of her body was that of a snake. She is also known as the mother of all monsters, because her children turned out to be quite the monsters in Greek mythology. She was married to Typhon. Typhon was rightfully her brother and a hundred-headed dragon. Given her looks and his, it is obvious that they would have had some very horrific children. And they had loads of them.

It is believed that both Echidna and Typhon were the children of Gaea and Tartarus. When the couple tried to fight against the Olympian gods, Zeus managed to overpower them. He buried Typhon under the volcanic Mount Etna while sparing Echidna and her children.

Echidna, however, met her doom at the hands of Argus Panoptes, who was the giant with a hundred eyes. She was murdered in her sleep.

Some of her children with Typhon were Cerberus (the dog with three heads), the Lernean Hydra (the serpent with multiple heads), the Gorgon sisters (Stheno, Euryale and Medusa) and Chimaera.

Giants

The giants were regarded as the epitomes of strength. When Cronus castrated his father, a few drops of his blood fell on the surface of the earth. The giants were said to have emerged from these blood drops. The Giants fought against the Olympian gods and goddesses. It was one of the most important wars in Greek mythology, second only to the war between the Titans and the Olympians. The reason for the outbreak of war between the Giants and the Olympians is unknown. However, the outcome of the war is certain; the Giants lost to the combined might of the Olympians and let the Olympians rule over them.

Some of the well-known giants were Eurymedon (the king of the giants), Porphyrion (the greatest of the giants) and

Enceladus (who suffered death at the hands of Athena by getting crushed under the island of Sicily).

Gorgons

The Gorgon sisters were the daughters of Echidna and Typhon. They were called Euryale, Stheno and Medusa. However, there is another myth that suggests that the parents of Medusa were Keto and Phorkys.

Euryale and Stheno were gifted with immortality, while Medusa was mortal. This discrepancy probably can be traced to the myth surrounding the parentage of Medusa. The Gorgon sisters had gruesome faces. Instead of hair, they had snakes entangled in coils on the tops of their heads. One gaze at their eyes was capable of turning anyone into stone instantly.

In fact, people are not well aware of Medusa having sisters, as only her story is very popular. The Gorgon sisters were extremely ugly and feared by all. They were the ones with beards and scary hair. They were made the guards of the underworld, as everybody feared them and it was the most suitable job for them.

Hekatonkheires

The Hekatonkheires were gigantic creatures. It is believed that they had fifty heads and a hundred hands. They were the children of Uranus and Gaea. There are three of them who are mentioned in the various literary accounts. These were Cottus (the striker), Briareus or Aegaeon (the sea goat) and Gyges (the big-limbed). The Hekatonkheires represented the natural forces of massive sea waves and the earthquakes.

Medusa

Medusa was one of the monsters of Greek mythology. She was one of the three Gorgon sisters. According to certain myths, Medusa was the daughter of Echidna and Typhon, whereas in other accounts she is believed to be the daughter of Keto and Phorkys, who were the children of Gaea and Uranus. One gaze at her eyes would turn anyone into stone. Even though she was the only mortal Gorgon, she was the deadliest of the lot.

The story of Medusa becoming what she was is a pretty tragic one. She was originally a fair maiden with golden locks and alluring eyes. She was a priestess in the temple of Athena and had taken a vow of celibacy. When Poseidon tried to win her heart, she fell for his charm, forgot about her vow, and ended up marrying him. This enraged Athena, and she decided to punish Medusa harshly. Her fair skin turned into a repulsive tinge of green while her golden locks turned into coiled snakes. Her alluring eyes turned bloodshot and were capable of stirring fear as well as disgust in the onlooker.

Everybody shunned Medusa for her gruesome appearance and drove her away. She finally decided to live up to their expectations. Because of the curse of Athena, she had the power to turn anyone into stone if they looked into her eyes. She terrorized people with this power. As we all know, she finally met her death at the hands of Perseus.

Pegasus

Pegasus was the white flying horse. His father was Poseidon and his mother was Medusa. His brother was Chrysaor. It was said that when Medusa was slain, Pegasus and Chrysaor were born.

Bellerophon captured and tamed Pegasus with the help of a magical bridle. Pegasus assisted him in many of his fights. He aided Bellerophon in defeating Chimaera. When Bellerophon decided to climb Mount Olympus on Pegasus, he was stopped by Zeus. However, Pegasus was allowed to fly on and reach Mount Olympus.

Sirens

The Sirens were beautiful creatures of Greek mythology. However, their beauty was just the bait to the traps they set. They were dangerous, vicious creatures. They were said to have huge teeth and transform into monsters pretty fast. They would again turn into beautiful maidens as soon as they had eaten their prey. Every time a ship would pass by their islands, they would lure the sailors on board with their beautiful voices. This was enough to distract the sailors and would result in the ships or boats crashing on the coral reefs. The Sirens were the daughters of Achelous, the river god. Even though they resided in a marine environment, they were not accorded the privilege of sea deities.

According to one myth, the Sirens were the companions of Persephone, the daughter of the goddess Demeter. Demeter had given each of the Sirens a pair of wings to take care of Persephone. However, when Hades abducted Persephone and took her to the underworld to marry her, Demeter was furious and cursed the Sirens. From then on, the Sirens sang a beautiful melody but it was laced with melancholy. It was said that the Sirens sang this song with the hope that Persephone would return someday.

There have been multiple tales of people encountering the Sirens amidst their journeys. When the Argonauts stumbled upon the Sirens *en route*, they were successful in evading them. Orpheus, who was travelling on board with the Argonauts, took out his lyre and started playing it. The music from his lyre blocked out the songs of the Sirens. Another interesting encounter with the Sirens is that of Odysseus. Odysseus advised his crew to plug their ears with wax and asked them to tie him to the mast of the ship and not to release him until they had passed the island. As expected, when they traveled near the island of the Sirens, Odysseus was allured by their songs. He begged his crew to untie him so that he could join the Sirens. The crew heard nothing because of the wax and started binding Odysseus with more rope. When the ship crossed the islands, Odysseus regained his conscious and was released from the mast.

Chapter 7:
Heracles and His 12 Labors

Heracles (also known as Hercules) was the son of Zeus and the mortal Alcmene and the most famous Greek hero of all time. Heracles faced 12 labors as an act of penance for slaying his wife and sons after being driven mad by Hera!

Originally, he was supposed to do ten labors as prescribed by King Eurystheus, but as two of his labors were rejected, he did two more. They were:

Nemean Lion

The Nemean Lion was a menace that kidnapped young women to lure heroes to save them. It is said that the lion was extremely brave and had a skin that was so tough there was no weapon on Earth that could pierce it. The skin and fur were just so thick that they could only be pierced by the lion's own claws. Heracles understood this and slew it using his bare hands. He managed to turn its claws on itself and kill it. He wore its fur as a protective coat of armor for the rest of his life.

Lernaean Hydra (a nine-headed monster)

This monster was raised by Hera to kill Heracles. The creature is said to have had a lion's head and the body of several snakes combined. This monster was next to impossible to kill, even for the world's strongest man, and there were many things that were stopping Heracles. There was a gigantic crab near the Hydra, which bit his toe and caused him immense pain. He finally managed to cut off its head, only to realize that two more were growing in its place. He was distraught and in bad shape. Heracles then solicited the help of his nephew, Lolaos, to defeat this monster, by burning the stubs of the decapitated heads to prevent regeneration. But since his nephew helped, this labor was rejected. However, Heracles was able to dip all his arrows in the Hydra's poisonous blood, which made them extremely potent and powerful.

Cerynian Hind

The next task was to capture the Cerynian hind. It belonged to Artemis. The Cerynian Hind was extremely fast, and even Artemis couldn't capture it. The hind would run at the speed of lightning and it would be extremely difficult to even lay a hand on it. Heracles found it quite tough, and yet he persisted. He eventually captured it as promised and returned it to Artemis. It is believed that the task took him one whole year, which completely tired the Hind out.

Erymanthian Boar

This task was very similar to the previous one and required Heracles to chase and capture the Erymanthian boar. The boar is said to run really fast and catching it was next to impossible. It again took Heracles a year to capture the boar. After taking advice from the centaur Chiron, Heracles captured the beast by driving it into thick snow. He is said to have tied its legs and taken it back on his shoulders. But in the process, he ended up piercing Chiron's body with one of his poisoned arrows.

Augean Stables

The Augean stables were full of excreta as the king of Elis, Augeias, had many cattle. The stable and the excreta were causing townspeople to get sick, and it was extremely important to have it cleared fast. Heracles was asked to clean it within a day after it had not been cleaned for 30 years. Heracles did so by digging a deep ditch on both sides of the stable and directing the river Alpheios inside to help clean it thoroughly. This labor was not counted as Heracles received payment for his services.

Stymphalian Birds

The Stymphalian Birds were man-eating birds with bronze beaks and were sacred to Ares. They were extremely tough to kill and it was impossible for one man to do it. Heracles used a gift he was given by Athena, a rattle made by Hephaestus, to scare them away and cause them to take flight. He was even able to shoot some of the birds with the poison arrows he had.

Cretan Bull

King Minos gave him permission to take the bull away as it was wreaking havoc in Crete. Heracles throttled it and shipped it back to Athens. There are doubts regarding what he did with the bull; he may or may not have killed it.

Mares of Diomedes

The mares were flesh-eating horses. Heracles first defeated Diomedes and then bound the mouths of the horses while they were eating and brought them back to Athens. It is believed that the horses were eating the body of either Diomedes or their grooms.

Belt of Hippolyta

This was a gift from Ares to the Queen of the Amazons, Hippolyta. She would have given the belt to Heracles anyway, but due to Hera's treachery, he was forced to kill her to get it. Hera had instructed the Amazons to treat heroes badly and possibly kill them on sight.

Cattle of Geryon

Geryon was a monster and was guarded by a two-headed dog named Orthrus and his herdsman Eurytion. Heracles killed both of them. He first shot Geryon with an arrow dipped in the venom of the Hydra, which killed him instantly. Heracles then captured Cattle. On his way, he is said to have put up markers, which then came to be known as the Pillars of Hercules.

Apples of the Hesperides

The Hesperides were the nymphs of the evening, and the dragon Ladon protected their golden apple tree. On his way there, Heracles came across Prometheus, who was tied to a gigantic rock, as punishment for having stolen fire from the gods. Zeus also sent a gigantic eagle to eat his liver on a daily basis. Heracles decided to kill the eagle, and to return the favor, Prometheus promised that his brother would help him by showing him the way to the Hesperides. Heracles wanted more and tricked Atlas into helping him by offering to hold up the sky while he snuck in to take the apples. Another story says he slew the dragon and took the apples himself.

Cerberus

Cerberus was the three-headed dog with the tail of a serpent that protected the entrance of the Underworld. With the help of Hestia, Hermes and Athena, Heracles entered Underworld while still alive. Hades said he could capture Cerberus on the condition that he did so without using any weapons. Heracles succeeded and slung the beast on his back and dragged it out of the Underworld. This is said to have been the toughest of tasks, as it was the last. Eurystheus is said to have chosen this task because he didn't want Heracles to complete it. When he saw that he had, Eurystheus was just so scared that he jumped into a jar and refused to come out.

This is how Heracles completed his 12 labors of penance. Heracles defeated many more monsters, and even journeyed with the Argonauts in search of the legendary Golden Fleece.

Chapter 8:
Important And Famous Women In Greek Mythology

In ancient Greek, the status and characteristic of women varied greatly. Further, historians agree that events in the history of Greece shaped the opinion and form of past and present women of Greece. In fact, according to Michael Scott, the best description of women in regards to their place in society and achievement is best by this quotation from Thucidydes:

"That the greatest glory for women is to be least talked about among men, whether in praise or blame."

I find this to be a warped view mainly because Greek history is full of women of great power, might, and achievement. Here are some of them.

Ariadne

Ariadne was the mortal daughter of King Minos and Queen Pasiphae of Crete. Ariadne aided Theseus when he came to slay the Minotaur by giving him a magical ball of yearn. As earlier indicated, Ariadne fell in love with Theseus but Theseus did not love her and abandoned Ariadne on an island where Dionysus found her and later married her.

Atalanta

The story of Atalanta is one of sadness especially in the early stage of her life. At a young age, she was left to die because no one knew the origins of her father and perhaps because her father wanted a son and the disappointment of a daughter was too great to bear. Her abandonment happened in Arcadia.

Story has it that a mother she-bear found her and decided to suckle her and raise her. She survived and lived with the bear until some hunters came along and brought her up. She grew up into a beautiful woman who swore to never marry; she would stay a virgin. She was a ferocious huntress and wrestler. Because she was also a warrior, she at one time asked Jason if she could accompany him on the Argo.

Calypso

Calypso was the daughter of the Titan Atlas and lived on the island of Ogygia where Odyesseus was washed up. Calypso fell in love with him and offered him eternal life if he could stay with her. He refused because of his wife Penelope. However, the two become lovers for seven years after which Athena complained to Zeus on behalf of Odysseus. Hermes was sent to Calypso to order her to release Odysseus. She reluctantly did so by helping him make a boat and escape from the island.

Charybdis

It is rumored that Charybdis was at one time a nymph. She was the daughter of Gaia and Poseidon. She flooded her father's underwater kingdom before Zeus turned her into a monstrous thing that sucked water in and out three times a day. Her home was a cave on the Sicilian side of the Straits of Messina, which was the monster Scylla and the two combining to form a real threat to any passing ship. In the Odyssey quest, Odysseus managed to avoid Charybdis.

The Charites

The Charites, also known as the Graces were triplets Goddesses of beauty. The first one was Aglaia, meaning splendor. The second one was Euphrosyne, meaning Mirth.

The third one was Thalia, meaning good cheer. The Charites were the first ones to welcome Aphrodite after the East Wind blew her to shore. Story has it that the these three rode in a chariot that was being pulled by white geese. The three were daughters of Euroynome and Zeus. In pre-classical mythology, they were goddesses of nature and fertility and had a close association with the underworld and the Eleusinian mysteries.

Circe

Circe was a cruel and evil sorceress. She had great power and turned Odysseus men into swine. Her powers included the power to cleanse and purify the Argonauts of the murder of Apysyrtus. If we were to translate her name, it would mean Falcon. She was the daughter of Perse and Helios.

Clytemnestra

She was the mortal daughter of Tyndareus, sister of Helen, Castor, and Polydeuces and Leda. Her husband was Agamemnon and she had four children, Orestes, Electra, Iphigenia, and Chrysothemia. After Agamemnon sacrificed Iphigenia to free Greek ship to go for the Trojan war, she never forgave him and while he was away, she plotted how to kill him with the help of her lover, Aegistus. When Agamemnon returned, Clymtemnestra killed him and Cassandra.

Demeter

Demeter was a daughter to Cronus and Rhea and was the goddess of the fields or the goddess of the harvest. In early Greek, citizens used to break bread in her name. She was mother to Persephone. She was very powerful. One time when Hades 'messed' with her, she let nothing grow and raged winter on earth until her daughter was found. Demeter and her daughter are very central to the Eleusian mysteries.

Draiads

Draiads were wood nymphs or nymphs of the forest. They were immortal and hunting companions to Artemis.

Echo

Echo is the most popular of all nymphs. Most argue that her voice and name live on to this date. She had a relationship with Zeus and lost her voice when she tried to protect Zeus from Hera's vengeance. She later fell deeply in love with Narcissus.

The Erinyes/furies

The furies conception happened when the Uranus blood was exposed to Gaia's body. They were fearful creatures older than any other Olympian gods. They were crones with snakes for hair, a dog's head, bat wings, coal-black bodies, and bloodshot eyes. They carried brass-studded scourges that gave their victims a ghastly death. They were three; Tisiphone, meaning the avenger, Megara, meaning the jealous, and Alecto meaning Un-resting. They bore the name the kindly ones or the Eumenides. Their job was to provide anguish and torment for the sinners on earth and Tartarus. Story has it that seeing one of the kindly ones could drive one to insanity. Initially, they only punished offenders of matricide, patricide, and breakers of oaths. Later on, they started punishing any sin. They lived in Erebus or darkness.

The fates

Parcae, Moerae, or the fates were the ones responsible for determining when life began, ended, and everything in between. The fates were three women:

- Lachesis- She appeared as a matron. She was responsible for measuring the thread of life. She was also the castor of lots.

- Clotho- She appeared as a maiden and was responsible for spinning the thread of life.

- Atropos- She appeared as a crone and was responsible for cutting the thread of life. She was the smallest in the group but was the most terrible.

The three of them were daughters of Erebus (darkness) and Nyx. There are those who believed that Zeus manipulated their decision. Mythically, they were eternal and powerful than any other gods. Further, there are those who believe that the three were parthenogenic daughters of Ananke.

The Gorgons

The Gorgons were three sisters with two of them being immortal. However, one of the sisters, Medusa was not. The three were daughters of Phorcys and Ceto. Their names were: Medusa, meaning ruler, Euryale, meaning far-roaming, and Stheno, meaning forceful. These three sisters were a remarkable sight. They were exceptionally beautiful and were rumored to turn anyone brave enough to stare them in the eyes into stone. They had golden-scaled bodies, and writhing and hissing snakes on their heads instead of hair. They had their sisters, the Graiae, as guards for their home beyond the sea.

The Graeae

The three grey sisters or the Graeae were beauties. They were said to be swan like and fair-faced. However, they had grey hair right from birth. Further, they shared one tooth and eye, which they lost when Perseus stole the eye and threw into a lake. The sisters names were: Deino, meaning terrible or dread, Pemphredo, meaning wasp or alarm, and Enyo, meaning war-like or horror. There are those who believe that the three were goddesses worshipped by the swan cults.

Helen

She who launched a thousand ships was also stunningly gorgeous. She was the daughter of Leda and Zeus and was immortal. Theseus abducted her when she was still a young girl, but her brothers rescued when Theseus was not around. Helen married Menelaus, brother to Agamemnon and had a daughter with him, Hermione. However, Paris came along and abducted her signaling the start of the war of Troy. After the war, she reunited with Menelaus.

The Muses

The Muses were nine. They were daughters of Mnemosyne and Zeus. They played the role of role of entertainers on Mount Olympus because they sang and danced all the time. They were also a source of creativity for the residents of Mount Olympus. The nine Muses were:

- Erato, the lyrical muse

- Euterpe, the musical muse

- #Thalia, the comical muse

- Melpomene, the tragedy muse

- Terpsichore, the choral song and dance muse

- Urania, the astronomy muse

- Clio, the muse of heroic and historical poetry.

- Polyhymnia, the hymns muse, and

- Calliope, the muse of epics.

Calliope, the last muse bore a child, Orpheus, for the king of Thrace. Further, the muses were individually great. For example, Clio introduced the Phoenician alphabet to Greece.

Thetis

Thetis was for a very long time the chief Nereid. In fact, she found Hephaestos as a baby after he was thrown out of Olympus. She then nursed him back to health. Zeus had a burning desire for her, but she rejected him. The goddess Themis had prophesied that she would give birth to a son stronger than his father would. Fearing this fate, Zeus was fearful and decreed that she should only marry a mortal. She became wife to Peleus and later mother to Achilles. She tried to make her son invisible but failed.

Scylla

Scylla was a beautiful maiden nymph and daughter to Ceto and Phorcus. As she was walking along the water edge one day, Glaucus, man turned sea-god, mottled her and lusted after her. However, she did not have any feelings for him. Circe, who was jealously in love with Glausus changed her into a monster that was human to the waist but the rest of her lower body were snapping and biting dogs. She moved to the Italian side of the Straits of Messina and ate anything that strayed in this area. In the Odyssey, Odysseus avoids Charybdis but Scylla gets seven of his men.

Persephone

From birth, Persephone was special. She was called Kore meaning maiden and was the daughter of Demeter. She was the goddess of the spring. While she was out picking flowers, the god of the underworld, Hades, abducted her, raped, and installed her as queen of the underworld. This role has earned her the title of being an unhappy and cold god. Her mother later rescued her from the underworld. However, she must return to the underworld annually.

These are just some of the more popular women in Greek mythology. This list does not cover all of them (we'll have to dedicate another book for that!). However, this just about covers the most important ones.

Chapter 9:
The Myth Of Sisyphus, The Most Cunning Of All Men

So, how can there be myths in Greek Mythology? Are they not the same thing? While most people consider ancient Greek to be a myth in itself, and rightly so, there are specific myths within the greater mythology. Let us look at some of these myths and mythologies.

The myth of Sisyphus

This myth is probably the most common and well-known myth in all of Greek mythology. This is perhaps because of the cunning nature by which Sisyphus cheated the punishment awaiting him. Sisyphus was a legendary rogue who cheated death twice. However, his cunningness and trickery caught up with him and he paid the ultimate price: eternal torture and suffering in the underworld.

Sisyphus was the son of Aeolus, king of Thessaly and Enarete. He had a brother, Salmoneus, and a wife, Merope, who bore him five sons, Sinon, Thersander, Glaucus, Omytion, and Almus. He was born as the heir to the throne of Thessaly, which was in central Greece. However, he and his brother, Salmoneus had a passionate hate for each other so the latter stole the throne from the former. Even though Sisyphus did eventually become king, he never became king of Thessaly. Instead, Medea, the sorceress gave him the throne of Ephyra. There are those who believe that he, Sisyphus, deserved the crown because he founded the city and allegedly populated it with people grown from mushrooms.

Homer called Sisyphus "the craftiest of men." He was extremely clever. A good example of this is when Autolycus grazed his cattle near his. Myth has it that Autolycus was a thief; he was so good at it that he stole anything he could lay his hands on without being caught. This is because he could change the color or form of whatever he stole. For example, if he stole white cows, he would change their color to brown. Using this trick, he would constantly steal cattle from Sisyphus herd. However, one time, Sisyphus noticed that some of his cows were missing and that those of Autolycus seemed to be increasing. However, he had no way of proving that Autolycus was guilty of theft.

To catch the thief, he marked the inside hooves of his cows. There are those who say that the marking was a message reading "Stolen by Autolycus" while others say that the message contained the letters "SS". Later, the marks were discovered on some of Autolycus cattle thus proving that he was a thief. Being the cunning person he was, Sisyphus did not get any satisfaction from proving that Autolycus was a thief. For his revenge, he seduced Autolycus daughter, Anticleia and later the mother of Odeysseus.

There are many other instances where Sisyphus used the daughter of an enemy to his advantage in taking revenge. At one point, he visited an Oracle at Delphi to find a way to exert revenge on his brother, Salmoneus. The oracle told him that if he bore children with his brother's daughter, the offspring's would destroy their grandfather. He therefore set out to have sex with his beautiful niece, Tyro. The words of the oracle did not happen because once Tyro learnt of it, she killed her two sons. Sisyphus cunningness did not stop there. Even though he stole, killed and raped, this is not what earned him a spot in the underworld. What earned him this 'honor' is his cunningness towards the gods.

His cunningness against the gods started with Zeus. Poseidon's offspring, Asopus, a river god was out looking for his daughter, Aegina after her disappearance. Sisyphus, who never shied away from anything that earns him favor promised to tell him what had happened to his daughter but only if the river god would create an eternal spring for his kingdom. After creating the stream, Asopus asked Sisyphus to tell him who had his daughter and Sisyphus named Zeus. Asopus, angry that Zeus had the audacity to kidnap his daughter pursued Zeus until Zeus's thunderbolts forced him to retreat. It is important to point out that Zeus has in fact taken the daughter. However, to punish Sisyphus for being a tattletale, Zeus sent Thanatos after him. However, being the cunning person he was, Sisyphus evaded death (Thanatos means death). Some say that he used some form of trickery to entrap Thanatos in heavy chains. After the lock up of death, people even extremely hurt, headless, mortally wounded people could not die and instead roamed the earth in pain begging for anyone for relief. Ares the war god later freed Thanatos and offered Sisyphus to him. This is not the only time that Sisyphus cheated a god. He also cheated Hades.

Before descending to Hades, Sisyphus left his wife instructions on how to bury him. She was to place a coin under his tongue (the coin was used to pay Charon, the transport for the dead as they made it across the river Styx on their way to the underworld home of the Hades), perform any necessary sacrifice to Persephone or Hades, and give him a proper funeral feast. It is in this state that Sisyphus arrived at the palace of Hades: as a pauper, an unburied one. He appealed to the queen Persephone by telling her that he was in the wrong place (he had no right being there) because he was an unburied one who did not have fare for the Charon. He told her that he should have been abandoned at the far side of the river Styx. Further, he argued that the neglect or failure of his wife to perform all the funeral rites, sacrifices, and ceremonies would set a bad precedence for other widows. He pleaded for a three-day opportunity to return to earth (its face) and arrange his funeral, punish his wife for her failure and teach her to respect the lords of the underworld. Undoubtedly, the queen fell for this ruse and allowed him to go home. Sisyphus who had no intention of keeping his promise renegaded and refused to go back after the three days lapsed. In fact, he lived for many years after this, until old age claimed him.

For his sins against Zeus and hades, he received eternal punishment in Tartarus, which was the lowest part of the underworld. Moreover, he was to roll a massive boulder to the top of a steep hill for all of eternity. After rolling hard and the stone almost reaching the top, the stone would roll back down again and he would have to start his labor from the start.

Chapter 10:
The Seven Wonders Of The Ancient World

The list of the seven wonders mainly comes from Greek myths and texts written by ancient Greek travelers and historians. This means that some difficulty may arise in separating the myths and the realities of these seven wonders.

Reality and Myth about the seven wonders of the ancient world

The seven wonders of the ancient world are not mythological in a sense. However, they have close association with various Greek heroes and myths. Further, these wonders later became grounds for other legends during other eras and years. The wonders were ancient architectural marvels. If we are to trust historians, the original list of seven, inclusive of Greek building was lost. The list as we know it now is a creation of the 3rd century BC, which articulate the fact that the Greek and barbarians could write fine pieces of work.

How the list was created

After Alexander the Great conquered, many people aka travelers who previously had no access to the ancient civilization of the Persians, Egyptian, and Babylonians found access easy. The beauty of the land at its marvels was breathtaking and the travelers fell in love with it. They therefore decided to list the sights and scenes as a way to remember all the places worth visiting. The ancient Greek word for these must-see sights in the ancient worlds was Theamata, loosely translating to must-sees.

The most popular of these lists, and the one we base our knowledge of these wonders is the list of Antipater of Sidon and an observer only identified as Philon of Byzantium. However, even with this list, it is impossible to know if all the wonders were real and not part of Greek myths. The seven wonders of the ancient world are:

- The hanging garden of Babylon

- The Lighthouse of Alexandria

- The Phidias' statue of Zeus in Olympia

- The Pyramids of Egypt

- The Colossus of Rhodes

- The mausoleum of Halicarnassus

- The temple of Artemis in Ephesus

Let us look at each of these wonders

The hanging gardens of Babylon

According to Diodorus Siculus, the hanging gardens of Babylon were multi-level and reached a height of up to 22 meters. They had an amazing module for water circulation. They were built by Nebuchadnezzar II by the banks of the River Euphrates as a gift to his wife Amytis of Media. Unfortunately, a massive earthquake destroyed the gardens in the 1st century BC. There is uncertainty on the facts about this garden and wanting questions on its existence. There is no evidence to show that it was not just a case of vivid imagination on the part of the ancient Greek especially considering that they had a flair for creating myths.

Phidias' Statue of Zeus in Olympus

The statue of Zeus occupied the entire width of the aisle of the temple of Olympia (specially built to house it) and was built in 466BC. The statue was 40 feet tall and made of ivory and gold. The Great Roman emperor Constantine ordered it disassembled and transported to Constantinople in the 4th century AD (Constantinople was the new capital of the Roman Empire). The statue was later destroyed in a great fire.

The Lighthouse of Alexandria

Built in the 2nd century BC, the lighthouse of Alexandria in Egypt was a 115-135 meter colossus. It was built on a small island at the entrance to the port of Pharos, later called the port of Alexandria (Pharos in Greek translates into lighthouse). The Lighthouse held the title for tallest building in the world for many years.

The Colossus of Rhodes

This Colossus is a gigantic depiction of the Greek sun god Helios. It was a very tall statue measuring about 110 feet and was located at the entrance of port Rhodes. If legend is anything to go by, the statue had one foot on either side of the harbor. A 226BC earthquake destroyed the statue a mere 56 years after construction.

The Pyramids of Cheops in Egypt

Built in 2,500BC, the Pyramid of Cheops or the Pyramid of Giza in Egypt was the oldest wonder of the seven world. It is the only one standing today. There is very little information on how these constructions took place. This has given birth to many legends and myths. The Pyramid was the tomb of King Cheops. It is also known as the Great Pyramid.

The Mausoleum of Halicarnassus

This mausoleum was approximately 135 feet tall. Each of the four sides had adornments of sculptural relief. Initially, the mausoleum was intended to be a tomb for Mausolus who was a Persian Satrap in 351. According to myth, the mausoleums' wealth was unbelievably big. It was later disassembled and destroyed when the crusaders entered Halicarnassus in AD1494.

The Temple of Artemis in Ephesus

The Greek city of Ephesus (Today in Turkey) played home to this temple. The temple was a dedication to the goddess Artemis. It took approximately 120 years to build. However, to achieve long lasting fame, Herostratus, a young Ephesian man, decided to burn it. It was rebuilt by Alexandra the Great but later destroyed by the Goths. It was rebuilt again in the 2nd century AD but later destroyed by St John Chrysostom in 401AD for being a pagan temple.

The list of the seven wonders of the ancient world has mutated over time. Subsequently, this list has inspired a new list of the seven wonders of the modern world.

Conclusion

This was a brief look at Ancient Greek mythology. By no means does this book contain all the myths, but it surely does touch upon the most important ones.

Greek mythology is extremely fascinating, with never a dull moment. Every story has a specific purpose to perform: either give a moral or explain some mystical phenomenon.

Take for example the story of Arachne. The story teaches the value of modesty and what a high price people with excess pride have to pay. It teaches everyone to believe that somewhere in the world, there is always someone better than them, and there is always room for improvement.

Similarly, as we explained, Persephone's yearly stint in the Underworld explains why there is a period of time that nothing grows (well, nothing grew in Ancient Greece – modern greenhouses have changed things a bit!).

Key Takeaways from This Book

Although myths are, as the term implies, stories, which are products of the imagination, they do offer us insights into the complex minds of the Ancient Greek philosophers who wrote them.

Greek myths are a reflection of the dynamics in that ancient society, because most of these stories were made to make sense of the world. From the rising and setting of the sun and tides, to the changing of the seasons, the Ancient Greeks had a relevant tale to tell.

The myths in the book also show that unlike the modern conceptions about God, the Ancient Greek gods and goddesses were fallible, capable of making mistakes, showing anger, greed, jealousy, and lust. This does not mean they were an inferior bunch – it only shows a different perspective people had way back then about religion and the divine.

Resources for Further Reading

http://en.wikipedia.org/wiki/Greek_mythology

http://www.mythweb.com/

http://www.greekmythology.com/

http://www.greekmythology.com/

http://www.history.com/topics/ancient-history/greek-mythology

Preview of Ancient Egypt: Discover the Fascinating World of Ancient Egyptian History, Myths, Pyramids and More!

Chapter 3: Myths of Egypt

Another intriguing aspect of Ancient Egypt is the various myths associated with it. These myths formed an integral part of the religion practiced in Ancient Egypt. On top of that, they found their way into the many literary texts, short stories, ritual texts and funerary texts that have been recovered from Ancient Egypt. In this chapter, we shall look at some of the more important Egyptian myths.

Creation

There are several myths surrounding the concept of creation. They vary in their accounts, especially when it comes to the deities involved in the creation of God. Each city and its priest espoused their own deity, and hence the deity involved in the creation of the world differed from city to city when the myth was retold.

According to these creation myths, the entire world emerged from the waters of chaos which surround it. The emergence of the world from the waters of chaos signifies the origin of life and the establishment of Ma'at. There is also a reference to the eight gods of the Ogdoad who signify the attributes of the primeval water. The actions of the eight gods result in the birth of the sun.

The birth of the sun is a source of light and dryness within the many layers of dark water in which the sun originates. The belief that the sun rises from the first mound of dry land is said to have been inspired by the sighting of the mounds of earth that emerge when the Nile flood recedes. Accordingly, the world's first ruler was the one who established the Ma'at.

However, the myths concerning the process of creation changed over the years. Later versions of the myths identified the creation as an intellectual process. Most of the creation myths dealt only with the creation of the universe; very few dealt with the creation of human beings. According to one of those few myths, the god Khnum shaped human beings from clay.

The Reign of the Sun God

According to the myths surrounding the sun god, Ra, the whole earth comprising both humans and gods was ruled by Ra. In the tradition of Egypt, this was considered as a golden age which represented stability and prosperity. Every ruler of Egypt sought to achieve the stability that was prevalent during the reign of Ra.

Another myth talks about a rebellion by other gods against Ra. Ra successfully destroys them with the help of other gods like Horus the Elder and Thoth.

As Ra grew older with the passage of time, human beings were believed to have plotted against his rule to take over the reign of the world. Initially, Ra decided to punish the rebelling human beings, but he later changed his mind and went on to pursue his journey through the Duat (the realm of the dead) and the heavens. The rebelling human beings were then attacked by the other human beings, which explains the origin of warfare and the destructive nature of human beings.

Osiris Myth

The myths concerned with Osiris are some of the most detailed and elaborate ones found to date. In the beginning of the myth, Osiris, who is the symbol of fertility and kinship, is believed to have been dismembered and scattered across Egypt. He is later restored to life through the efforts of his sister and wife, Isis. The process by which Osiris is revived represents the Egyptian traditions in connection with embalming and burial.

Isis and Osiris give birth to the god Horus, whose life is threatened by Set, Osiris' brother. Isis tries to protect her son from the barbs of Set and is considered the epitome of maternal love.

When Horus competes with Set to claim the throne, one of his eyes is torn out. However, it is restored by the healing powers of Thoth. Since Horus is the god of the skies, one eye represents the sun and one eye represents the moon. It was believed that the reason why the moon is less bright than the sun was because that was the eye that got injured during the battle.

After Horus becomes the sole ruler and restores order, the funerary rites he performs give Osiris a new life in the Duat. Hence, Osiris is considered the symbol of regeneration in Egyptian mythology. He becomes the sole ruler of the Duat. On earth, Osiris is believed to be the reason behind the growth of crops every year; in the Duat, Osiris is the reason behind the rebirth of the sun.

The Journey of the Sun

Of the many stories that surround the journey of the sun god, Ra, the most widespread one is this:

As Ra travels across the skies on his way to the Duat, he illuminates the whole world with his light. His strength is at its maximum when it is noontime, declining as the day goes by and his light fades at the beginning of the sunset. The stars that adorn the night sky are the gods that were gobbled up by Ra at sunrise and later spit out at sunset. Since the sun sets in the west, it was believed that the horizon on the western sky holds the door to the Duat. It was also believed that the sky goddess Nut swallowed Ra to facilitate his journey through the Duat.

Another important myth that surrounds the journey of Ra is the meeting of Osiris and Ra. When Ra meets with Osiris, they combine to form a single being. This combination reflects the Egyptian ideology about the repeating patterns of time, with Osiris being the static member and Ra being the dynamic one. Osiris' power of regeneration gives Ra enough strength to continue with his journey. This is said to have been the reason behind Ra emerging at dawn in the sky with renewed energy, thereby bringing light to the world. At this juncture, Ra swallows the stars to regain more energy to help him during his journey.

Birth of the Royal Child

Many myths refer to the child of God who is the ultimate heir to the throne. The earliest of these stories were told as folktales instead of as myths. According to the oldest folktale, the first three kings of the Fifth Dynasty were the children of Ra and a human woman. This myth found its way into many other stories to project different kings as true heirs to the throne. Divine birth legitimizes the king's claim to the throne and lays down the rationale for the belief that a Pharaoh is a messenger of God himself.

Another example of this myth resurfacing in the New Kingdom is the depiction in the temple reliefs of Amenhotep III, Hatshepsut and Ramesses II claiming that their father is the god Amun and their mother is the historical queen. These myths were basically aimed at giving a mythical flavor to the coronation of the king.

One common aspect in all these myths was the capability of the son of God to restore order in the kingdom and ensure stability.

End of the Universe

The universe ending was considered a highly unlikely event, and hence very few texts throw light on the process of the dissolution of the universe. According to one of the myths, Atum, the oldest god, will dissolve the world and return it to the primitive state it was in before emerging from the waters of chaos. Only Atum and Osiris would survive this event. However, the hope of another creation still exists because the universe was created from the waters of chaos as well as being destroyed therein.

[Click Here to Download Ancient Egypt: Discover the Fascinating World of Ancient Egyptian History, Myths, Pyramids and More!](#)